This is for Nanna. And Preston. And
scraped knees. And ashy elbows.
I love y'all.

—G.G.

To my big brothers,
Onye and Bosa

—O.M.

Balzer + Bray
is an imprint of HarperCollins Publishers.

I'm From
   Text copyright © 2023 by Gary R. Gray, Jr.
Illustrations copyright © 2023 by Oge Mora
All rights reserved. Manufactured in Italy.
No part of this book may be used or reproduced in any manner whatsoever without written permission
except in the case of brief quotations embodied in critical articles and reviews. For information address
HarperCollins Children's Books, a division of HarperCollins Publishers, 195 Broadway, New York, NY 10007.
www.harpercollinschildrens.com

Library of Congress Control Number: 2022951818
ISBN 978-0-06-308996-9

The artist used acrylic paint, gouache, china markers, colored pencils, tissue paper, an airbrush,
pastels, patterned paper, and old book clippings to create the illustrations for this book.
Hand lettered by Oge Mora. Designed by Dana Fritts.
23 24 25 26 27 RTLO 10 9 8 7 6 5 4 3 2 1

First Edition

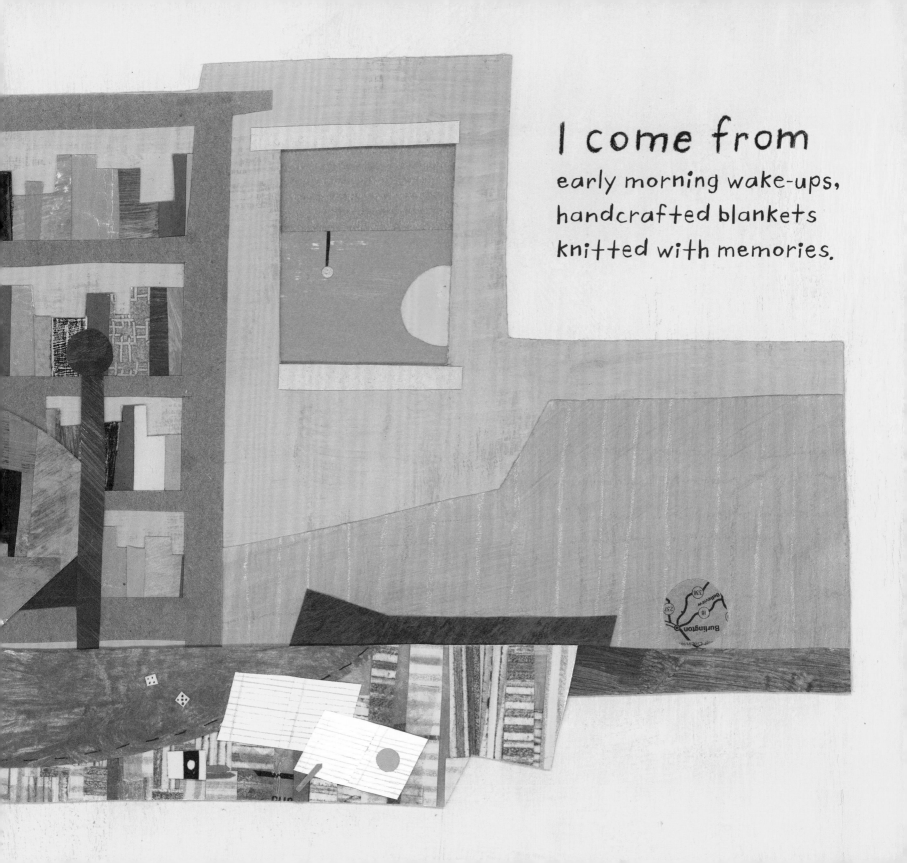

I come from
early morning wake-ups,
handcrafted blankets
knitted with memories.

Is that my favorite?
Pan-fried bologna,
homemade pancakes,
strawberry jam.

Cotton candy hair
and razor-sharp
lineups.

High fades and
low fades,

tight ponytails

and laid edges.

What's up, y'all?

rumbling

RATTLING

Good morning beats,

hip-hop and   vibrating seats,   and   sunrise dancing,

Four square,
hoop dreams,
grounders,
double Dutch, and
freeze tag.

Too soon
morning whistles.

I come from l⬚⬚⬚⬚⬚ng school days.

Sky-high bookshelves,
dusty classics.

Books that don't

click

with me;

one or two that do.

And the
other kids.

.......can I touch your HA

.....you don't sound BLA

......do you play BASKETBA

I'm from
    notebooks,
       stubby pencils,
  drawing my own heroes,
  writing
      my own stories.

caramel candy squares,
butterscotch buttons,
Tootsie Rolls.

From
leftovers,
buttermilk biscuits,
baked beans,
    and
You better eat
what's on your plate.

Bear-tight cuddles,
late-night belly laughs,
taking turns,
  and rolling dice.
Is it bedtime already?

Moon as a night-light,
soft pecks on the cheek.

Sleep tight, and remember, you're from...

I come from somewhere.